再遇
傲慢与偏见

爱与人生的微妙交响

[英] 简·奥斯汀 著　人间书 译　非晚 绘

人民邮电出版社

北京

图书在版编目（CIP）数据

再遇傲慢与偏见：爱与人生的微妙交响 /（英）简
•奥斯汀著；非晚绘；人间书译. -- 北京：人民邮电
出版社，2025. -- ISBN 978-7-115-66240-8

Ⅰ. I561.074

中国国家版本馆 CIP 数据核字第 20256A8T87 号

内 容 提 要

200多年前，英国作家简•奥斯汀在《傲慢与偏见》中告诉年轻的男孩女孩：不要仅凭外表判断一个人；只考虑金钱的婚姻是荒谬的，不考虑金钱的婚姻是愚蠢的……书中的至理名言随着时光流逝，历久弥新。

无论你是反复阅读《傲慢与偏见》仍感觉意犹未尽的"简粉"，还是想快速领略简•奥斯汀文学经典的"新手"，这本书都是你的不二之选。本书精心筛选了《傲慢与偏见》中的关键情节及经典语录，并按照故事发展的顺序巧妙串联——5分钟，就能为你带来不一样的治愈与感动；特别采用中英双语设计，最大程度保留原著风格；除了动人的对白，更有唯美的英式田园风光插图……相信本书会为你带来一场视觉与情感的饕餮盛宴。

◆ 著　　　[英] 简•奥斯汀
　　绘　　　非　晚
　　译　　　人间书
　　责任编辑　朱伊哲
　　责任印制　周昇亮

◆ 人民邮电出版社出版发行　　北京市丰台区成寿寺路 11 号
　　邮编　100164　电子邮件　315@ptpress.com.cn
　　网址　https://www.ptpress.com.cn
　　天津裕同印刷有限公司印刷

◆ 开本：690×970　1/24
　　印张：6　　　　　　　　2025 年 4 月第 1 版
　　字数：83 千字　　　　　2025 年 4 月天津第 1 次印刷

定价：34.90 元

读者服务热线：(010)81055296　印装质量热线：(010)81055316
反盗版热线：(010)81055315

Love is the dawn after abandoning pride and prejudice.

爱是摒弃傲慢与偏见之后的曙光。

译者序

"傲慢让别人无法爱上我，偏见让我无法爱上别人。"

——《傲慢与偏见》

爱情是永恒的话题，始于初见时的那一抹心动，终于精神上的携手并进。

但人与人之间的误解和偏见，使得许多爱情在萌芽期就无奈凋零。

在一段感情里，如果傲慢与偏见一直存在，悲剧将会屡次上演。

伊丽莎白一直认为达西先生傲慢无礼，自己又何尝不是心怀偏见呢？

幸而，两颗心愿意跨越重重阻碍，坦诚相待，去向对方靠近。

爱情，在达西先生坚定地裹着一腔爱意和真诚，于晨雾中缓缓走来时，彻底绽放……

人间书

Main characters

主要人物

伊丽莎白·贝内特

本书的女主人公，家中排行第二。聪明、独立，有很强的自尊心，和姐姐简最为亲密。

达西

本书的男主人公，出身名门望族，仪表堂堂，非常富有。一开始表现得冷漠傲慢，在伊丽莎白的影响下逐渐改变，并解开了彼此之间的误会。

简·贝内特

伊丽莎白的姐姐，作为家中长女的她情感内敛，对人满怀善意。大家都说她是贝内特家中最漂亮的女儿。

宾利

达西的好友，有钱的单身汉，对贝内特家的大女儿简一见钟情。热情、率真，十分敬重达西，凡事总爱听取他的建议。最后与简结婚。

贝内特先生

伊丽莎白的父亲，有五个漂亮女儿的乡绅。睿智、幽默，总爱用反讽的语言打趣妻子。在所有女儿中最偏爱伊丽莎白。

贝内特太太

伊丽莎白的母亲，整天操心着为女儿们物色称心如意的丈夫。举止浅薄，总爱拿自己敏感的神经说事儿。

威廉·柯林斯

贝内特家的远房亲戚，古板平庸，善于谄媚，依靠凯瑟琳夫人的权势当上了牧师。因为贝内特家没有男性继承人，按照当时的法律，他将继承贝内特家的家产。他向伊丽莎白求婚遭拒绝后，马上与她的密友夏洛特结婚，这也给伊丽莎白带来了不少烦恼。

夏洛特·卢卡斯

伊丽莎白的密友，懂得很多道理却也为自己的终身大事担忧。她的爱情观和伊丽莎白截然不同。在伊丽莎白拒绝柯林斯的求婚后，夏洛特最终为了利益嫁给了柯林斯。

威克姆

备受女士们喜爱的漂亮军官，达西儿时的玩伴。表现得绅士风趣，实则是个唯利是图的人。为了报复达西，到处传播毁谤他的谣言，让伊丽莎白对达西产生偏见。后来与伊丽莎白的妹妹私奔，在大家都手足无措的时候，达西默默出面解决了问题。

凯瑟琳夫人

达西的姨妈，柯林斯的庇护人。为人傲慢，极其看重阶级地位。一心想让自己的女儿嫁给达西，并蛮横地要求伊丽莎白保证不与达西结婚。

有钱的单身汉总要娶位太太，这是一条举世公认的真理。

It is a truth universally acknowledged, that a single man in possession of a good fortune, must be in want of a wife.

贝内特太太的人生大事，是把女儿们嫁出去；她的人生乐事，是访亲拜友和打听消息。

"我亲爱的贝内特先生，你听说内瑟菲尔德庄园终于租出去了吗？"
"对方叫什么名字？"
"宾利。"

"My dear Mr. Bennet, have you heard that Netherfield Park is let at last?"
"What is his name?"
"Bingley."

"他是已婚还是单身？"

"哦！当然是单身！一位年收入四五千英镑的富有单身汉。这对我们的女儿们来说，是多好的事情啊！"

"Is he married or single?"

"Oh! single, my dear, to be sure! A single man of large fortune; four or five thousand a year. What a fine thing for our girls!"

"那又如何？这跟女儿们有什么关系？"

"我亲爱的贝内特先生，"他的妻子回答道，"你怎么这么讨厌！你要知道，我正在考虑让他娶她们中的一个呢。"

"How so? How can it affect them?"

"My dear Mr. Bennet," replied his wife, "how can you be so tiresome! You must know that I am thinking of his marrying one of them."

其实，贝内特先生早就有计划去拜访宾利先生。直到他从内瑟菲尔德庄园回来，贝内特太太才知道实情。

"你就喜欢气我，一点都不体谅我那脆弱的神经。"
"你误会我了，亲爱的。我非常尊重你的神经。它们是我的老朋友啦。至少在这二十年里，我总是听见你提起它们。"

"You have no compassion on my poor nerves."
"You mistake me, my dear. I have a high respect for your nerves. They are my old friends. I have heard you mention them with consideration these twenty years at least."

在大家期待的目光中，宾利一行人首次现身舞会。

宾利先生仪表堂堂，气质优雅，面容和善，举止洒脱……然而，他的朋友达西先生的到来立刻引起了全场的瞩目。他那高挑的身材、俊朗的面庞和高贵的气度无不让人赞叹；在他入场后的短短五分钟内，关于他年收入一万英镑的消息便迅速在舞池中传播开来。

Mr. Bingley was good looking and gentlemanlike; he had a pleasant countenance, and easy, unaffected manners...but his friend Mr. Darcy soon drew the attention of the room by his fine, tall person, handsome features, noble mien; and the report which was in general circulation within five minutes after his entrance, of his having ten thousand a year.

人们差不多有半个晚上都带着爱慕的目光看着他，直到他的举止引起众人厌恶，人们最后才发现他傲慢自负、目中无人、对与周围人社交毫无兴趣。即便他在德比郡拥有丰厚的产业，也无法掩饰他那阴沉而令人不快的面容，**况且他和他的朋友比起来，更没有什么大不了的**。

He was looked at with great admiration for about half the evening, till his manners gave a disgust which turned the tide of his popularity; for he was discovered to be proud, to be above his company, and above being pleased; and not all his large estate in Derbyshire could then save him from having a most forbidding, disagreeable countenance, and being unworthy to be compared with his friend.

宾利和简跳了几次舞，整个人快活极了。他走出舞池，想要达西跟着一起跳，坐在不远处的伊丽莎白听到了他们的谈话。

"你说的是哪一位？"达西说着转过身，朝伊丽莎白望了一会儿，直到伊丽莎白的目光与他相遇，他才移开视线，冷冷地说道："**她还算说得过去，但是还没漂亮到能够打动我的心。眼下，我可没有兴致去抬举那些受到别人冷落的小姐。**"

"Which do you mean?" and turning round, he looked for a moment at Elizabeth, till catching her eye, he withdrew his own and coldly said, "She is tolerable; but not handsome enough to tempt me; and I am in no humour at present to give consequence to young ladies who are slighted by other men."

如果说原先伊丽莎白对达西有些许赞赏和热情，此刻已荡然无存。

舞会后，简对伊丽莎白诉说自己对宾利的爱慕之情，伊丽莎白感叹道：

"你从来看不到别人身上的缺点。在你眼中，整个世界都是善良而可亲的。我这辈子从未听你说过别人的坏话……假装坦诚、道貌岸然的人比比皆是，但能做到坦诚、不张扬、不算计，善于发现每个人的优点并赞不绝口，而对其缺点绝口不提的——只有你。"

"You never see a fault in anybody. All the world are good and agreeable in your eyes. I never heard you speak ill of a human being in my life... Affectation of candour is common enough;—one meets it every where. But to be candid without ostentation or design—to take the good of every body's character and make it still better, and say nothing of the bad— belongs to you alone."

伊丽莎白去拜访密友夏洛特·卢卡斯，询问她对达西的看法。

"他骄傲，"卢卡斯小姐说道，"但不像一般人骄傲那样让我反感，因为他实在有理由。想想看，这么出色的一个小伙子，门第好，又有钱，具备这么多优越的条件，难免自视甚高。要我说呀，他的骄傲是完全合情合理的。"

"His pride," said Miss Lucas, "does not offend me so much as pride often does, because there is an excuse for it. One cannot wonder that so very fine a young man, with family, fortune, every thing in his favour, should think highly of himself. If I may so express it, he has a right to be proud."

"这倒一点不假，"伊丽莎白答道，"假使他没有伤害我的自尊，我会很容易原谅他的骄傲。"

"That is very true," replied Elizabeth, "and I could easily forgive his pride, if he had not mortified mine."

简深深爱上了宾利，却仍表现得十分内敛、娴静。作为旁观者的卢卡斯小姐对伊丽莎白表达了自己的看法。

"如果一个女人巧妙地隐藏了自己对某人的爱慕，她可能会错失搞定他的良机。这样一来，即便她自以为瞒过了所有的人，那也不过是自我安慰罢了……略有好感本是很自然的事情，**但是很少有人能在没有受到对方鼓励的情况下，敢于倾心相爱**。"

"If a woman conceals her affection with the same skill from the object of it, she may lose the opportunity of fixing him; and it will then be but poor consolation to believe the world equally in the dark...a slight preference is natural enough; but there are very few of us who have heart enough to be really in love without encouragement."

"要和一个人过一辈子，最好尽量少了解他的缺点。"

"It is better to know as little as possible of the defects of the person with whom you are to pass your life."

伊丽莎白全神贯注地注视着宾利先生对她的姐姐献殷勤，一点也没有注意到，宾利的这位朋友渐渐对她留起神来。

达西起初几乎不觉得她漂亮；在舞会上，他看向伊丽莎白时，毫无爱慕之情；当他们再次相遇时，他的目光只为挑剔而来。然而，就在他向自己和朋友们坚定地表示她几乎没有什么优点时，却意外地发现，那双乌黑的眼睛如此让人着迷，使她整个人看起来极其聪颖。

Mr. Darcy had at first scarcely allowed her to be pretty; he had looked at her without admiration at the ball; and when they next met, he looked at her only to criticise. But no sooner had he made it clear to himself and his friends that she had hardly a good feature in her face, than he began to find it was rendered uncommonly intelligent by the beautiful expression of her dark eyes.

受邀前去内瑟菲尔德庄园做客的简病倒了，伊丽莎白十分担心，急忙去看望她。

"一个女人在齐踝的泥浆里孤零零地跑了三英里、四英里、五英里，谁知道多少英里！她到底是什么意思？依我看，这表明她狂妄放肆到令人作呕的地步，一点体面也不顾，乡巴佬气十足……我恐怕，达西先生，"宾利小姐低声怪气地说道，"她这次冒失的行为或许大大影响了你对她那双美丽眼睛的喜爱之情吧？"

"毫无影响，"达西答道，"经过一番奔波，她那双眼睛越发明亮了。"

"To walk three miles, or four miles, or five miles, or whatever it is, above her ancles in dirt, and alone, quite alone! What could she mean by it? It seems to me to shew an abominable sort of conceited independence, a most country town indifference to decorum...I am afraid, Mr. Darcy," observed Miss Bingley, in a half whisper, "that this adventure has rather affected your admiration of her fine eyes."

"Not at all, " he replied; "they were brightened by the exercise."

为了方便照顾简，伊丽莎白在内瑟菲尔德庄园暂住。

达西先生也在此处。随着进一步地交流，伊丽莎白越来越笃定自己对他的第一印象是正确的。

"我做任何事情都是匆匆忙忙的，"宾利说道，"所以如果我决定离开内瑟菲尔德，恐怕五分钟内就能走人。不过，眼下我打算在这儿住定了。"

"我也是这么猜想的——我完全了解你。"伊丽莎白说。

"Whatever I do is done in a hurry," replied he; "and therefore if I should resolve to quit Netherfield, I should probably be off in five minutes. At present, however, I consider myself as quite fixed here."

"That is exactly what I should have supposed of you. I understand you perfectly." said Elizabeth.

"我希望我能把这当作一种赞美，但如此容易被看穿，我恐怕显得很可悲。"（宾利）

"确实如此。**不过，一个性格深沉而复杂的人，未必比你这样的人更值得尊重。**"（伊丽莎白）

"I wish I might take this for a compliment, but to be so easily seen through I am afraid is pitiful."

"That is as it happens. It does not necessarily follow that a deep, intricate character is more or less estimable than such a one as yours."

"**我一向认为，诗是爱情的食粮。**"（达西）

"对那种美好、坚贞、健康的爱情来说，确实如此。世间万物都能滋养那些本已强烈的感情。但若仅是一点微弱、脆弱的倾慕，我相信一首优美的十四行诗就能将它彻底扼杀。"（伊丽莎白）

"I have been used to consider poetry as the food of love."
"Of a fine, stout, healthy love it may. Every thing nourishes what is strong already. But if it be only a slight, thin sort of inclination, I am convinced that one good sonnet will starve it entirely away."

"虚荣心的确是个弱点。可是骄傲——只要有了真正的聪明才智，骄傲总是会受到很好的控制。"（达西）

伊丽莎白转过身去，忍住不笑。

"Vanity is a weakness indeed. But pride—where there is a real superiority of mind, pride will be always under good regulation."

Elizabeth turned away to hide a smile.

"我想，我的性情不能委曲求全——确实不太符合世俗。我无法迅速忘记他人的愚蠢与过错，也无法轻易释怀别人对我的冒犯。我的情绪也不是随意就能激发起来。我的脾气可以说是不饶人的。**我对人一旦失去好感，便永远没有好感**。"（达西）

"It is I believe too little yielding—certainly too little for the convenience of the world. I cannot forget the follies and vices of others so soon as I ought, nor their offences against myself. My feelings are not puffed about with every attempt to move them. My temper would perhaps be called resentful. —My good opinion once lost is lost for ever."

"我相信，每个人的性格中都会有某种短处，即使你受到最好的教育，也还是克服不了。"（达西）

"你的缺点是好怨恨人。"（伊丽莎白）

"你的缺点么，"达西笑着答道，"就是成心误解别人。"

"There is, I believe, in every disposition a tendency to some particular evil, a natural defect, which not even the best education can overcome."

"And your defect is a propensity to hate every body."

"And yours," he replied with a smile, "is wilfully to misunderstand them."

达西对伊丽莎白的好感日渐强烈，他决定用理智压制情感。

为了谨慎起见，他决定要特别当心，绝不让任何爱慕之情流露出来，亦不容她心生希望，以为她能左右他的终身幸福……即便他俩曾独处半小时，他也始终认真地埋头于书中，瞧也没瞧她一眼。

He wisely resolved to be particularly careful that no sign of admiration should now escape him, nothing that could elevate her with the hope of influencing his felicity...and though they were at one time left by themselves for half an hour, he adhered most conscientiously to his book, and would not even look at her.

伊丽莎白听闻威克姆对达西人格的贬低后，想亲自去验证。

"达西先生，我记得有一次听你说过，你一旦跟人结了怨，心生的怨恨就再也消除不掉。我想，你与人结怨的时候一定很谨慎吧。"

"是的。"达西坚定地说道。

"Mr.Darcy, that you hardly ever forgave, that you resentment once created was unappeasable. You are very cautious, I suppose, as to its BEING CREATED. "

"I am. " said he, with a firm voice.

"从来不受偏见的蒙蔽？"（伊丽莎白）

"我想不会。"（达西）

"And never allow yourself to be blinded by prejudice?"

"I hope not. "

在后来的内瑟菲尔德庄园舞会上，伊丽莎白意识到自己家人的表现有多么不得体。

看到母亲对着那位卢卡斯夫人在毫无忌讳地信口乱说，大声谈论她是如何期待简与宾利先生迅速成婚的事情，让伊丽莎白越发气恼。她们对这件事越聊越起劲，贝内特太太一个劲儿地一一列举这桩婚事的种种好处。

Deeply was she vexed to find that her mother was talking to that one person (Lady Lucas) freely, openly, and of nothing else but of her expectation that Jane would be soon married to Mr. Bingley. It was an animating subject, and Mrs. Bennet seemed incapable of fatigue while enumerating the advantages of the match.

她忍不住不时地偷偷瞥向达西先生，每看一眼都让她愈加忐忑：因为他虽然不总是盯着她母亲看，但她确信，他的注意力总是不由自主地被她母亲吸引。**他脸上先是显出气愤和厌恶的表情，慢慢地变得冷静庄重，一本正经。**

She could not help frequently glancing her eye at Mr. Darcy, though every glance convinced her of what she dreaded; for though he was not always looking at her mother, she was convinced that his attention was invariably fixed by her. The expression of his face changed gradually from indignant contempt to a composed and steady gravity.

贝内特家族的继承人柯林斯到访，表示想娶家中一位女儿作为自己的妻子，好弥补自己的亏欠。伊丽莎白坚决拒绝了柯林斯的求婚。

"我可不是第一次听说，"柯林斯先生刻板地挥了挥手，继续说道，"年轻的女士常常会拒绝别人的第一次求婚，即使心里想要答应，而且，有时还会拒绝第二次甚至第三次。因此，我绝不会因为你刚才的话而感到气馁，我期盼不久后就能和你在教堂举行婚礼。"

"I am not now to learn," replied Mr. Collins, with a formal wave of the hand, "that it is usual with young ladies to reject the addresses of the man whom they secretly mean to accept, when he first applies for their favour; and that sometimes the refusal is repeated a second, or even a third time. I am therefore by no means discouraged by what you have just said, and shall hope to lead you to the altar ere long."

得知柯林斯求婚，贝内特先生和贝内特太太有着截然不同的反应。

"伊丽莎白，你面临着一个不幸的抉择。从今天起，你要和你父母中的一个形同陌路了。如果你不嫁给柯林斯先生，你的母亲将再也不见你；而如果你嫁了，我也将永远与你断绝关系。"（贝内特先生）

"An unhappy alternative is before you, Elizabeth. From this day you must be a stranger to one of your parents. Your mother will never see you again if you do not marry Mr. Collins, and I will never see you again if you do."

宾利在达西的劝说下离开了内瑟菲尔德庄园。

简对宾利先生的离开表示释怀，伊丽莎白愤愤不平地说道：

"**对这个世界看得越多，我就越不满**。每天的经历都让我更加相信，人性是多么矛盾，那些表面的优点和智慧实在不值得信赖。"

"The more I see of the world, the more am I dissatisfied with it; and every day confirms my belief of the inconsistency of all human characters, and of the little dependence that can be placed on the appearance of either merit or sense."

"我并不认为宾利先生的行为有什么用意，"伊丽莎白说，"但如果不是故意做错事或让别人不高兴，依然可能会出错，给别人造成痛苦。凡是粗心大意、无视别人的感受、优柔寡断，都一样会坏事。"

"I am far from attributing any part of Mr. Bingley's conduct to design," said Elizabeth; "but without scheming to do wrong, or to make others unhappy, there may be error, and there may be misery. Thoughtlessness, want of attention to other people's feelings, and want of resolution, will do the business."

威克姆得知伊丽莎白不能继承家产后，对她的殷勤也随之告终，他把目标换成了别人。

伊丽莎白留心观察着一切，她虽然看得清楚，也写进了信里，却并未感到多大的痛苦。她只有些轻微的触动，虚荣心也得到了满足，因为她相信，若非财产的问题，她本该是他唯一的选择。

Elizabeth was watchful enough to see it all, but she could see it and write of it without material pain. Her heart had been but slightly touched, and her vanity was satisfied with believing that she would have been his only choice, had fortune permitted it.

她安慰自己道：

"太受人器重有时需要付出昂贵的代价。美貌青年与相貌平常的人一样，也得有饭吃，有衣穿。"

"Importance may sometimes be purchased too dearly. Handsome young men must have something to live on as well as the plain."

卢卡斯嫁给柯林斯后，伊丽莎白去看望他们，同时收到了凯瑟琳夫人的邀请，准备动身前往罗辛斯庄园。

"亲爱的表妹，别为你的衣着感到不安。凯瑟琳夫人根本不要求我们穿得像她和她的女儿那样华丽。我建议你只穿上那些比其他衣服稍好一些的就行了，没必要过于讲究。凯瑟琳夫人不会因为你穿得简单而对你有任何看法，她喜欢保持身份的差别。"（柯林斯）

"Do not make yourself uneasy, my dear cousin, about your apparel. Lady Catherine is far from requiring that elegance of dress in us, which becomes herself and daughter. I would advise you merely to put on whatever of your clothes is superior to the rest, there is no occasion for any thing more. Lady Catherine will not think the worse of you for being simply dressed. She likes to have the distinction of rank preserved."

凯瑟琳夫人身材高大、五官分明，年轻时也许很漂亮。她的气质冷漠，接待客人时的态度更是让人无可避免地感受到身份的差距。她默不作声的时候倒不那么吓人，但她说话时那种威严的语气，无不彰显出她的自命不凡。

Lady Catherine was a tall, large woman, with strongly-marked features, which might once have been handsome. Her air was not conciliating, nor was her manner of receiving them such as to make her visitors forget their inferior rank. She was not rendered formidable by silence; but whatever she said was spoken in so authoritative a tone as marked her self-importance.

不久，凯瑟琳夫人的外甥达西也到访罗辛斯庄园。当伊丽莎白为大家弹奏钢琴时，达西走过来注视着她。

"达西先生，你这副架势走来，莫非是想吓唬我吧？尽管令妹（达西的妹妹，是一位远近闻名的才女）确实弹得很出色，但我也不害怕，**我这个人生性倔强，绝不肯让人把我吓倒。越是想来吓唬我，我的胆子就越大。**"

"You mean to frighten me, Mr. Darcy, by coming in all this state to hear me? But I will not be alarmed though your sister does play so well. There is a stubbornness about me that never can bear to be frightened at the will of others. My courage always rises with every attempt to intimidate me."

"我弹起琴来，"伊丽莎白说，"手指不像许多女人那样灵巧娴熟。既不像她们那么有力，那么灵巧，也不像她们弹得那么有感觉。不过，我一直认为这都是我的问题——因为我不愿意去花时间练习。并不是我不相信自己能像其他女性一样，演奏得如此出色。"

"My fingers," said Elizabeth,"do not move over this instrument in the masterly manner which I see so many women's do. They have not the same force or rapidity, and do not produce the same expression. But then I have always supposed it to be my own fault—because I would not take the trouble of practising. It is not that I do not believe my fingers as capable as any other woman's of superior execution."

达西笑笑说："你说得完全正确。可见你的练习效率比别人高得多。凡是有幸听过你演奏的人，都不会觉得还有什么不足之处。我们两个人都不愿在陌生人面前表现自己。"

Darcy smiled, and said, "You are perfectly right. You have employed your time much better. No one admitted to the privilege of hearing you，can think anything wanting. We neither of us perform to strangers."

伊丽莎白从别人口中得知，是达西拆散了宾利和简。

"我实在不明白达西先生凭什么有权决定他朋友的心意，或者为什么他要单凭自己的判断来左右他人该如何追求幸福。"（伊丽莎白）

"I do not see what right Mr. Darcy had to decide on the propriety of his friend's inclination, or why, upon his own judgment alone, he was to determine and direct in what manner that friend was to be happy. "

伊丽莎白拿出简最近写给她的信，想象着达西做过的种种，仿佛要进一步激发自己对他的厌恶。突然，门铃响了起来——是达西先生。

沉默了几分钟后，达西激动地走到她面前，开始说道："我内心的挣扎是徒劳的，这样不行，我再也无法压抑自己了。请允许我告诉你，我是多么仰慕你，多么爱你。"

After a silence of several minutes, he came towards her in an agitated manner, and thus began, "In vain have I struggled. It will not do. My feelings will not be repressed. You must allow me to tell you how ardently I admire and love you."

伊丽莎白惊讶到一时说不出话来。她虽然厌恶他，但心想能得到这样一个人的爱慕，也不能不觉得是一种恭维。但随着达西提到觉得她出身低微、感到内心矛盾，她的悲悯化作了愤怒：

"我相信一般人碰上这种情形，都会表示感激，但我无法这么做。我从来没有渴求你的赞许，而你显然也是非常勉强的。很遗憾我造成了你的痛苦，但我完全是无心的。"

"In such cases as this, it is, I believe, the established mode to express a sense of obligation for the sentiments avowed. But I cannot. I have never desired your good opinion, and you have certainly bestowed it most unwillingly. I'm sorry to have occasioned pain to any one, but it has been most unconsciously done."

伊丽莎白的回答远远超出达西的预想。他这时正倚靠在壁炉旁，显得又惊奇又气愤。一阵沉默后，达西故作镇定地说道：

"这就是我所能期待的全部回应吗？也许我想知道，为什么我会遭到如此无礼的拒绝。不过，这都不重要了。"

"And this is all the reply which I am to have the honour of expecting! I might, perhaps, wish to be informed why, with so little endeavour at civility, I am thus rejected. But it is of small importance."

"你为什么要这样如此露骨地冒犯我，侮辱我，非要告诉我你是违背自己的意志、理智甚至人格而喜欢我？"（伊丽莎白）

"Why, with so evident a design of offending and insulting me, you chose to tell me that you liked me against your will, against your reason, and even against your character?"

"我完全有理由这么想你。没有任何动机能为你扮演的不公正和无情的角色开脱。你不敢，也不能否认，你就是让他们分开的主要原因，甚至是唯一的原因——让一个人因为反复无常而受到世人的谴责，让另一个人因为希望破灭而受到世人的嘲笑，让他们俩都陷入了极度的痛苦之中。"（伊丽莎白）

"I have every reason in the world to think ill of you. No motive can excuse the unjust and ungenerous part you acted there. You dare not, you cannot deny that you have been the principal, if not the only means of dividing them from each other—of exposing one to the censure of the world for caprice and instability, the other to its derision for disappointed hopes, and involving them both in misery of the acutest kind."

"我并不想否认，我确实尽力想让我的朋友和你的姐姐分开，而且我为自己的成功感到高兴。我对他的关心甚至比对我自己还要多。"（达西）

"I have no wish of denying that I did everything in my power to separate my friend from your sister, or that I rejoice in my success. Towards him I have been kinder than towards myself."

"从一开始——几乎可以说是从我认识你的第一刻起，你的举止让我深信你的傲慢、你的自负，你对他人感情的冷漠自私。这些都是我不喜欢你的理由，后来发生的事情更是使我对你产生了不可动摇的厌恶。认识你不到一个月，我就意识到，你是这个世界上我绝对不会说服自己去嫁的人。"（伊丽莎白）

"From the very beginning—from the first moment, I may almost say—of my acquaintance with you, your manners, impressing me with the fullest belief of your arrogance, your conceit, and your selfish disdain of the feelings of others, were such as to form that groundwork of disapprobation on which succeeding events have built so immoveable a dislike; and I had not known you a month before I felt that you were the last man in the world whom I could ever be prevailed on to marry."

"您说得够多了，女士。我完全理解您的感受，现在，我只为自己的感情而感到羞愧。请原谅我占用了您这么多时间，希望你健康、幸福。"（达西）

"You have said quite enough, madam. I perfectly comprehend your feelings, and have now only to be ashamed of what my own have been. Forgive me for having taken up so much of your time, and accept my best wishes for your health and happiness."

伊丽莎白心烦意乱，痛苦不堪。等达西走后，她大声哭了起来。

第二天，她决定去林间小路透透气，只见达西先生急急忙忙地向她走来。

这时他也走到了她面前，递出一封信，伊丽莎白本能地接过。达西面带一抹傲然的淡定，缓缓说道："我在树林中徘徊了很久，期待能遇见你。您能赏光读一下这封信吗？"说罢，他微微一鞠躬，转身走入树林，瞬间便消失在了她的视线中。

He had by that time reached it also, and, holding out a letter, which she instinctively took, said, with a look of haughty composure, "I have been walking in the grove some time in the hope of meeting you. Will you do me the honour of reading that letter?" And then, with a slight bow, turned again into the plantation, and was soon out of sight.

小姐:

当你收到这封信的时候,请不要担心这封信里会再次出现昨晚那些令你厌恶的感情或提议。我写这封信,并不想使你难过,也不想自讨没趣,为了我们各自的幸福,我应该尽快忘掉那些心愿……请原谅我冒昧地占用你的时间;我知道你的感情是不情愿的,但是我要求你公正地对待我……

看完信后，伊丽莎白才知道，原来是因为简面对宾利波澜不惊的表现引起了误会，同时自己家人粗俗的言行也让达西意识到这不是一桩合适的婚姻。

在信中，达西对自己片面的判断表示道歉，同时也列举了威克姆的卑劣行为，包括将达西先父赠与他的财产挥霍一空后，便想带着达西的妹妹私奔，万幸的是，他们在最后关头被达西发现并拦下。

"我竟然如此自负！"伊丽莎白大声叫道，"我还一向自鸣得意地认为自己有眼力、有见识呢！我还常常看不起姐姐的宽怀大度，为了满足自己的虚荣心，总是任意猜疑他人。这真让我感到羞愧啊！"

"How despicably have I acted!" she cried, "I, who have prided myself on my discernment! —I, who have valued myself on my abilities! I, who have often disdained the generous candour of my sister, and gratified my vanity, in useless or blameable distrust. —How humiliating is this discovery!"

"起初认识他们两个的时候，我因为一个人的偏爱而感到得意，因为另一个人的冷落而心生不满。在这两件事上，我既喜欢先入为主，又那么无知。直到此刻，我才有点自知之明。"（伊丽莎白）

"Pleased with the preference of one, and offended by the neglect of the other, on the very beginning of our acquaintance,I have courted prepossession and ignorance, and driven reason away, where either were concerned. Till this moment, I never knew myself."

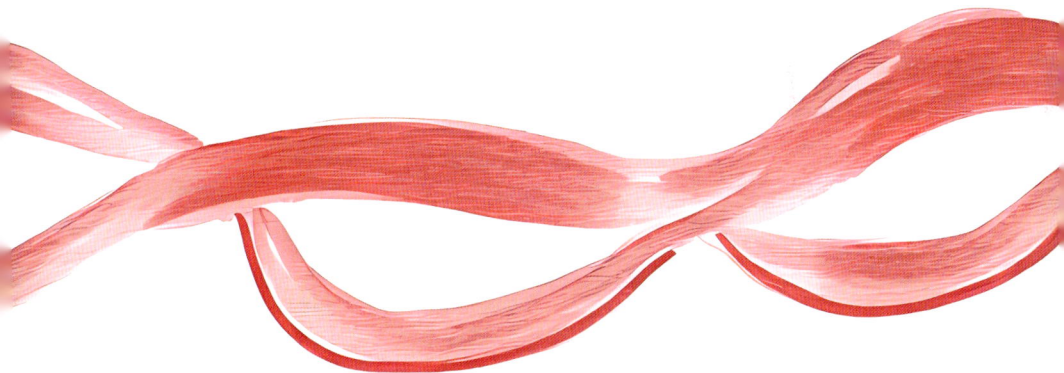

伊丽莎白回到家后，迫不及待地告知简威克姆的真实面目（当然，为了避免简伤心，有关宾利先生的事她一句没提）。

"可怜的威克姆，他的脸上透着如此善良的神情！他的举止是多么真诚温和！"（简）

"这两个年轻人的教育显然存在着严重问题。一个人拥有真正的善良，而另一个人则只有善良的外表。"（伊丽莎白）

"Poor Wickham; there is such an expression of goodness in his countenance! Such an openness and gentleness in his manner!"
"There certainly was some great mismanagement in the education of those two young men. One has got all the goodness, and the other all the appearance of it."

为了排解心中的烦闷，伊丽莎白决定随舅舅和舅妈北上旅行。

他们正好路过富丽堂皇的彭伯里庄园（达西的宅邸），这里的美景全国闻名。在得知达西不在家中后，伊丽莎白终于放下心跟随大家去参观，并从女管家口中得知了大家对达西的真实看法。

"如果您的主人愿意结婚，您就能经常见到他了。"（伊丽莎白的舅舅）

"是的，先生；但我不知道那要等到什么时候。我真不知道谁能配得上他。"（女管家）

"If your master would marry, you might see more of him."
"Yes, sir; but I do not know when that will be. I do not know who is good enough for him."

"他是世上最好的庄主，也是最好的主人，"她说道，"可不像如今那些狂妄的年轻人，只知道为自己着想。他的租户或佣人，没有一个不愿为他说好话的。有些人说他傲慢，但我可瞧不出来。在我眼中，他只是不像别的年轻人那样喋喋不休罢了。"

"He is the best landlord, and the best master," said she, "that ever lived; not like the wild young men nowadays, who think of nothing but themselves. There is not one of his tenants or servants but what will give him a good name. Some people call him proud; but I am sure I never saw anything of it. To my fancy, it is only because he does not rattle away like other young men."

"您不觉得我们少爷非常英俊吗，小姐？"
"是的，非常英俊。"

大家穿过草地，朝河边走去。就在伊丽莎白转头的当间，忽然看见屋主人从通往马厩的大路上走了过来。达西出现得突然，根本让人来不及躲闪。顿时，他们的目光交会，脸都涨得通红。

随后，达西反应过来，走到客人面前，和伊丽莎白寒暄。他对待舅舅和舅妈也彬彬有礼，热情又不失分寸。

如此傲慢的一个人，竟会发生这般变化，这不仅让伊丽莎白感到惊奇，也让她为之感激——这只能归根于爱情，炽烈的爱情。这种爱情尽管让她捉摸不透，但她决不感到讨厌。她尊敬他，器重他，感激他，真心实意地关心他的幸福。

Such a change in a man of so much pride excited not only astonishment but gratitude—for to love, ardent love, it must be attributed; and as such its impression on her was of a sort to be encouraged, as by no means unpleasing, though it could not be exactly defined. She respected, she esteemed, she was grateful to him; she felt a real interest in his welfare.

此刻，她开始领悟到，达西无论从性情还是才华方面，都是最适合自己的那个人。尽管他的智慧和性情与自己的截然不同，却能满足她所有的愿望。这样的结合对双方都将大有裨益：女方大方活泼，可以柔化他的心性，使他的举止更为优雅；男方见多识广，精明通达，也必将给她带来很大益处。

She began now to comprehend that he was exactly the man who, in disposition and talents, would most suit her. His understanding and temper, though unlike her own, would have answered all her wishes. It was an union that must have been to the advantage of both; by her ease and liveliness, his mind might have been softened, his manners improved, and from his judgment, information, and knowledge of the world, she must have received benefit of greater importance.

回到旅馆后，伊丽莎白收到了简的来信：家中的小妹妹竟然与威克姆私奔了！这让伊丽莎白十分崩溃，达西对此也感到十分震惊。在安慰过伊丽莎白后，他匆匆离开了。

"我本可以阻止这一切的！我明明知道他是什么样的人。要是我能向家里人透露一点——哪怕只透露我了解到的一部分真相就好了！要是他的品行早为人知，这种事就不可能发生。但现在，说什么都——太晚了。"

"that I might have prevented it! I, who knew what he was. Had I but explained some part of it only—some part of what I learnt, to my own family! Had his character been known, this could not have happened. But it is all—all too late now."

伊丽莎白匆匆回到家，妹妹和威克姆终于被找回来了——他们打算结婚，虽然伊丽莎白和简为此表示担忧，但贝内特家族其他人都松了一口气。

尽管达西先生极力保持低调，伊丽莎白还是得知，原来是他私底下找到威克姆，并给了对方很大一笔钱和好的职位，才化解了危机。

伊丽莎白知道达西拆散宾利和简的原因后，告诉达西简对宾利的深情。达西意识到自己的错误，决定帮助宾利和简重新走到一起。

在双方明确彼此的心意后，宾利向简求婚，简欣然答应。

大约在宾利和简订婚后的一个星期，凯瑟琳夫人突然造访。她进屋后，冷冰冰地对伊丽莎白说：

"贝内特小姐，我非要听你说个明白。我的外甥向你求过婚没有？"

"Miss Bennet, I insist on being satisfied. Has he, has my nephew, made you an offer of marriage?"

"夫人您已断言此事绝无可能。"

"理应如此，必须如此，只要他尚有一丝理智。但你有使不完的花招，或许在他一时的心迷意乱中，让他忘却了对自己以及全家的责任。你可能已经让他深陷其中了。"

"我即使把他迷住了，也决不会说给你听。"

"Your ladyship has declared it to be impossible."

"It ought to be so; it must be so, while he retains the use of his reason. But your arts and allurements may, in a moment of infatuation, have made him forget what he owes to himself and to all his family. You may have drawn him in."

"If I have, I shall be the last person to confess it."

"要是达西先生既没有义务，也不愿意跟他表妹结婚，那他为什么不能另做选择？**要是他选中了我，我为什么不能答应他？**"

"If Mr. Darcy is neither by honour nor inclination confined to his cousin, why is not he to make another choice? And if I am that choice, why may not I accept him?"

凯瑟琳夫人回去对达西痛斥了伊丽莎白的无礼行为，却万万没想到，伊丽莎白的话竟然重新燃起了达西再次向她求婚的希望。

"你是个有肚量的人，不会耍弄我。**要是你的态度还和四月时一样，就请你立即告诉我。我的感情和心愿依然如故**。不过，你只要发句话，我就永远不提这件事。"（达西）

"You are too generous to trifle with me. If your feelings are still what they were last April, tell me so at once. My affections and wishes are unchanged, but one word from you will silence me on this subject forever."

伊丽莎白深感他当前处境的尴尬与焦虑远超往常，不得不强迫自己开口。她虽说得不够流利，却立刻告诉他，自那时以来，她的情感已发生了巨大的变化，以至于她如今能满怀感激与喜悦地接受他。

Elizabeth feeling all the more than common awkwardness and anxiety of his situation, now forced herself to speak; and immediately, though not very fluently, gave him to understand that her sentiments had undergone so material a change, since the period to which he alluded, as to make her receive with gratitude and pleasure his present assurances.

这句话给他带来的幸福也许是他以前从未感到过的，他在这个场合表现得理智而热烈，就像一个热恋中的男人所能表现出来的那样。

The happiness which this reply produced was such as he had probably never felt before, and he expressed himself on the occasion as sensibly and as warmly as a man violently in love can be supposed to do.

131

倘若伊丽莎白能抬起头来看看他那双眼睛，她就会发现，他满脸洋溢着的喜悦使他显得越发英俊。不过，尽管她没有把目光移向他，却能听到他的声音。他向她诉说着衷肠，表明她对他来说是多么重要，也让他的爱意每时每刻都变得更加珍贵。

Had Elizabeth been able to encounter his eye, she might have seen how well the expression of heartfelt delight, diffused over his face, became him; but, though she could not look, she could listen, and he told her of feelings, which, in proving of what importance she was to him, made his affection every moment more valuable.

两人不管什么方向，只顾往前走。

他们有多少事情要思索，要体味，要谈论，哪还有心思去注意别的事情。

"你必须学点我的哲学。只记住那些让你愉快的回忆就足够了。"（伊丽莎白）

"You must learn some of my philosophy. Think only of the past as its remembrance gives you pleasure."

"我虽然不主张自私，可事实上却自私了一辈子。小时候，大人只教我什么是对的，却不教我如何控制自己的脾气……要不是多亏了你，最亲爱、最可爱的伊丽莎白，我可能到现在还是那个样子！真是多亏了你！你教训了我一顿，开头真让我有些受不了，却让我受益匪浅。"（达西）

"I have been a selfish being all my life, in practice, though not in principle. As a child I was taught what was right, but I was not taught to correct my temper...and such I might still have been but for you, dearest, loveliest Elizabeth! What do I not owe you! You taught me a lesson, hard indeed at first, but most advantageous. "

散步的时候，二人决定晚上去征得贝内特先生的同意。

"我真的，真的喜欢他，"她眼含泪光回答道，"我爱他。其实，他并没有那么傲慢。他非常和蔼可亲。您不了解他真正的为人，所以请不要再用那种话来说他，以免让我难过。"

"好吧，亲爱的，"等她停止说话时，贝内特先生说道，"我就不再多说了。如果真是这样，那他配得上你。"

"I do, I do like him," she replied, with tears in her eyes; "I love him. Indeed he has no improper pride. He is perfectly amiable. You do not know what he really is; then pray do not pain me by speaking of him in such terms."

"Well, my dear," said he, when she ceased speaking, "I have no more to say. If this be the case, he deserves you."

"我真是太高兴了——太快活了。他多么迷人啊！——如此英俊！个子还那么高！——哦，我亲爱的莉齐（对伊丽莎白的爱称）！请原谅我之前那么不喜欢他。希望他能既往不咎。亲爱的，亲爱的莉齐。"（贝内特夫人）

"I am so pleased—so happy. Such a charming man!—So handsome! So tall!—Oh, my dear Lizzy! Pray apologise for my having disliked him so much before.I hope he will overlook it. Dear, dear Lizzy."

伊丽莎白写给舅妈的信：

我现在成了天下最幸福的人。也许别人以前也说过这句话。可是谁也不像我这样名副其实。我甚至比简还要幸福，她只是莞尔而笑，而我却是开怀大笑。达西先生将爱我之心分享出一部分，向您表示问候。

"I am the happiest creature in the world. Perhaps other people have said so before, but not one with such justice.I am happier even than Jane, she only smiles, I laugh. Mr. Darcy sends you all the love in the world that he can spare from me."

项目统筹：许文瑛　徐竞然

策划编辑：朱伊哲

文字编辑：王钰博

美术指导：谭李彤　郝俊泽